THE GATOR PIT

THE DEFENSE

It was fun—a needed distraction in the last period of a long school day. And she was such an easy target! An inviting target! Hey, in our minds she might as well have worn a bull's-eye on her shirt, and every direct hit would have been deserved. In fact, all considered, we had been downright merciful. Pretty harmless stuff, really. And what's more, we'd been subtle enough not to get caught in the act.

~

"The Gator Pit should be required reading for all students before entering high school."

— Barbara Gondek, Ph.D.
Department of Education
UNH at Manchester

Former Curriculum Coordinator for Language Arts & Social Studies K-8, Bedford, NH School District

J. Morneau

THE GATOR PIT

Stonegate Publishing

Cover artist – Lindsey Gillis 2010
Cover design – gillisgrafix 2010

ISBN   1452882223

EAN – 13   9781452882222

Stonegate Publishing
Londonderry, NH
© 2010 J. Morneau All Rights Reserved
Printed in the United States of America

This book is dedicated to my many hundreds of students, each of whom taught and inspired.

~Acknowledgments~

~Thank you to my supportive manuscript readers with their invaluable professional input:

… my husband Roland, daughter Tracey Gamache, and sister Carol Shaw

… my early mentor, author Tom Fitzgerald, whose support was critical in getting me started

… my ever ready consultant, Joanne O'Connor

… and my other advocates – Peter Gaucher, Kiki Harrington, Meg Hartnett, Susan Mast, Dylan Newell, Cindy Petherbridge, Ann West, and my final copy editor, Maureen Comfort

~Thank you to those who gave steady encouragement:

… Sandy Nolan, Rita Sullivan, and Ginny True

~Thank you to Dick Keller for sharing a bit of his humor

~Thank you to Tod and Kathy Wicker who connected me to my first professional reviewer, Carolyn W. Field

~Thank you to Ryan Gamache, David Gillis, and Mark Stevens for their technical assistance

~ Contents ~

Prologue

Graduation Day at Barton High School – June 10, 2000

For an afternoon we are one. First our stream of blue and white flows into a block, then into a time warp that shifts us between past and future and eventually onto the doorstep of a new millennium.

We are told by our commencement speaker to learn from our mistakes and not to fear failure. But he forgets to mention that some mistakes should never have been made—those that came at too high a price when we should have known better.

When the blue and white rows blend into a single line, I scan the faces of the graduates, and I find him. I give him a thumbs-up. He answers with a nod. I am glad he is here and glad for whoever

1

helped him arrive. I could not have been one of them. I think of who is *not* here.

I watch my 400 plus classmates do their solo brisk walks across the platform—except for my friend who labors across with a nagging limp. He receives a diploma *and* a standing ovation. For a whole minute the rhythm of the ceremony is broken, and it is awesome.

When all diplomas have changed hands, the tassels mark the moment as they sweep across our mortarboards like hands being moved along the face of a clock.

Then come the cheers, photos and celebrations.

My mental images of blue and white may soon fade, but I know the images of freshman year will not. My inner clock hands return to those, and they are as sharp and clear as if they happened yesterday. They begin with family.

Chapter One

FARE WELL — NOT

As sister and brother, Tracey and I had our share of spats, but after putting maple syrup in her shampoo bottle and *really* ticking off the teen queen wannabe, I knew that this time I had gone too far. With her long dark hair and fit figure, she was hot, and my guy friends, always hoping for a Tracey sighting, never let me forget it. If only they could see her now, standing at the top of the stairs, wrapped in a robe and foaming at the mouth over stiffened hair strands that had all the appeal of flypaper. They'd think I'd dumped ice water on her.

"Just 'cuz *you* don't care if you look like a frazzled sea cucumber," she bellowed, referring to my own head full of thick dark curly sprigs. This became the target as she hurled the bottle of sweetness, but my quick hands spared the walls around me.

Lately she was overreacting to just about anything on the planet—probably uptight about the business of choosing a college. "Calm down," I urged, and then added lamely, "Just think. When you're gone in a few months, I'll be out of your hair for good."

But my parents weren't about to wait that long. After the hair prank they decided I wasn't mature enough for the campus scene, so instead of taking Tracey *and* me to look at colleges during the school break, they dropped me off to stay with my aunt and uncle. "A good chance to get to know Aunt Lucy and Uncle Ted," my parents assured me. That was adult talk for "*No way are we leaving YOU alone to trash the place.*" Besides, my staying home alone, or even better, staying at a friend's house would be a reward. They weren't into rewards right now, and

I had that figured out in a nanosecond when my parents led me into my aunt and uncle's house.

My uncle rose unsteadily from his chair. Bent at the waist, he held on to the chair's arm with one hand while gesturing a "hello" with the other. He collapsed back, red-faced and breathless. His chair, molded to his plump body shape, sank under his weight. Looking around the room at other prissy chairs, I knew the one he sat in was the only one up to the task. A metal walker and a table lined with medicine bottles stood nearby.

Married to this slug was the energizer bunny. Aunt Lucy and chairs didn't sit well. She dashed in to greet us wearing a swirly dress that couldn't stay still, a hairdo that couldn't move, and heels that could nail me to the floorboards. She gagged me with perfume vapors. I suddenly missed the scent of Mom's Lysol.

"We'll take good care of Tod," my aunt assured my parents as she looked me up and down. Her chest rose with a deep breath as her eyes settled on my hair.

Stuck by itself on a winding road to nowhere, their house wasn't anything like our small, busy house in the suburbs surrounded by similar small, busy houses. Theirs was big and formal—like a funeral home. Had it one lousy basketball net, their place might have scored a two out of ten. My only baskets, however, were in grocery stores and musty antique shops for dragging in my aunt's goods while Uncle Ted stayed home and rested up for his next nap. Lucky for Uncle Ted she liked antiques because he was ancient.

Not lucky for me, however. By each day's end, I was given a torturous house tour of her "museum pieces," a bunch of paintings and vases mixed in with a prized glass paperweight collection "worth a small fortune," she said. Had the tour not been my gofer "reward," I was convinced she would have charged a fee. Her stuff didn't excite me at all, but I figured something like an ancient skull or a stuffed wolverine would have added a nice touch.

After spending the first couple of mornings watching her shine the shine on everything but the bald spot on my Uncle Ted's head, I began to take a strong dislike to her useless ornaments.

On my third morning I woke early enough to inspect the downstairs without a tour guide. I stopped at the paperweights on my way to the kitchen and stared into one of the crystal balls to see if I could figure out why it was worth "a small fortune." A puny lizard tucked under a flower. Not my idea of a showstopper. I picked it up and casually tossed it in the air a couple times. On the next toss I saw all too clearly my *own* fortune as it slipped from my fingers, struck the corner of the brick hearth, and shattered on the wood floor. I scrambled to pick up the broken petals and lizard, now belly-up and encased in shards of glass.

Aunt Lucy could scramble too, and before I could remove the telltale evidence, she appeared at the doorway dressed in a flowing robe. She looked like the Statue of Liberty gone mad. If the torch had been in her hand instead of a fistful of white knuckles, I would have been seared. "*Hey, lady!*" I thought to myself. "*What do you think a kid does when he sees a fist-sized round object? He tosses it. It's reflex."*

But this time both my voice and my reflexes failed me. I couldn't even mumble, "It was just an accident." In an instant my rating slumped from her "fine young man" (which was a crock anyway) to a "damn kid." No way was any apology coming from me.

For the next few days until my parents returned, I was banished to the outdoors. Through the window I could see Aunt Lucy armed with bottles, mops, and sponges, scrubbing away all signs of my existence. Like I cared. I could easily pull my own vanishing act by hiding away in her potting shed. There, I scanned magazines of babes and cars I'd "borrowed" from the grocery store while Aunt Lucy had her nose up to every melon she could get her hands on.

When my parents arrived, they'd never looked better. I noticed how lean and tall my Dad stood, and I really dug the worn elbows of his faded flannel shirt and his paint-spattered sneakers. I liked my Mom's windblown hair and lint-covered jacket. And her over-the-top hug told me she'd missed me.

Soon after, however, I wondered if they too would have gladly wiped out my existence. I could hear mumblings of disgust and occasionally make out words like *priceless, rude,* and *those magazines* from Aunt Lucy's kitchen where Tracey and three adults had gathered.

Meanwhile, I sat with Uncle Ted. I noticed the spark in his eye when I stood up and studied a picture of a proud young man in uniform standing next to a Coast Guard cutter. "I could tell you some stories about those days," Uncle Ted said. But tales of ocean rescues were too soon drowned out by my parents' stern voices demanding my apology. I offered one up reluctantly.

Mom and Dad hauled me home in hours of silence, hardly a fitting treatment, I figured, after spending four days at "the morgue."

"So, how was college, Trace?" I asked, friendly-like as we finally rolled up our driveway.

She slammed the car door and clicked her heels along our front walk. "They don't have babysitters for people like you, little brother," she hollered without looking back.

"Great to be on home turf," I muttered, sinking against the back seat of the car. "Stiffville was friendlier than this."

I'd hit a nerve. My father turned to look at me from the driver's seat, barking out the corner of his mouth.

"You'll see a lot of your home turf in the next few days. You're grounded. Again! And if live stuff is what you want, your jungle that you call a bedroom is crawling with it."

Jungle to them; to me it was nirvana. I found it the way I had left it—old socks, t-shirts, gym shorts and sneakers on the floor, all smelling of body workouts and team battles; my favorite pair of jeans—torn, grease-stained, and strewn over a pile of clean laundry; my CD's and wadded up balls of paper everywhere. Above my stale half-eaten jelly sandwich hung my favorite local rock group, The

Demons. In my mind they were playing a song celebrating home, *my* home, with no precious crystal balls to show off my own recklessness and to predict more shattering to come.

Chapter Two

AND NOW THERE ARE FOUR

Just as I felt that I was about to choke on rules, my grounding was lifted, and Mole appeared at my house. He was about as *un*ruly as they come and a welcome sight. His real name was William Moulton. His friends called him Mole. He was the first of our big four I'd seen since arriving home, but that wasn't unusual. He always liked to be number one.

"Hey, man," Mole said as he put me in a headlock.

"Stick it, Mole," I grunted, straining and jabbing at his rib cage. I shot upright and kneed him in the chest. Taller than Mole, I sometimes had the edge on him even though he was stronger.

Small and wiry, Mole had muscled his way into my life the first day I met him at the town field where he sided with me on a disputed call at first base and set off a brawl. Brawling was a habit with him, and yielding to Mole's one-sided play calls became a habit of others. Knowing that, I made a point of playing on *his* teams and soon became his go-to guy.

Now I watched his jaw tighten. "Easy, Mole." I gave him a mock jab to his shoulder. Like many others, I too had to be wary of him.

And for a good reason. Mole could be brutal. In hockey he didn't care if he drew blood with his high-sticking and boarding. He didn't even care if he sidelined a kid for the season. He was proud of his league-leading time spent in the penalty box. When his old man, a beefy loud-talking guy, bought Mole new clubs and took us out on the links to introduce him to the more serene game of golf, Mole went ballistic. While he mastered "shanking," "club toss" became the name of the game. Clubs, fairways, greens—they all took a pounding. Yet there were times I couldn't have cared less about his outbursts. Like when I was the designated caddy until no longer in view of the clubhouse. Then I'd become a player with a free round, compliments of Daddy Moulton.

Mole also had this thing about fear. He liked to cause it. After giving the fairways a break, we were both soon armed with tennis rackets, compliments of Daddy Moulton again. At first Mole used his to pelt tennis balls at younger kids until they surrendered to us the town court which was rightfully theirs. The kids scattered like birds at a turkey shoot, leaving behind their jackets, racket covers, tennis balls—whatever was not attached to them when we arrived. We'd scored without a match! With time it got even better as kids took off before Mole took aim. Yet the ending was always the same. With all muscle and no finesse, Mole's game would quickly regress into his launching balls over the court's tall fence while ignoring the net and lines. Then with the strut of someone who had just experienced the thrill of victory, he'd lead us off the court. I would have liked more playing time but said nothing and pretended to share in the rush.

When Mole wasn't taking aim at a puck or a ball, he'd be gunning the engine of his father's Firebird and roaring up and down his driveway. "Home-schooled Driver's Ed.," he called it. "Cheap, fast, and easy." It turned nasty the day he decked his older brother, Alex. Alex had spilled the story to his friends about Mole's attempt to act cool by backing "the bird" into their garage with his driver's side front door wide open and his head leaning out to look behind him. The back half of the car and his head cleared, but Mole managed to take out his open car door, buckling it against the front fender. As Mole told it, Alex, like so many others he'd taken down, had simply gotten "what he deserved."

I saw it differently. An excuse to beat up on Alex couldn't have come soon enough for Mole. Alex—the solid B student—the star athlete—the one well liked by teachers and coaches—the class rep—everything Mole was *not* and claimed he didn't want to be. To Mole, Alex played "the game" and sold out to the system. It wasn't that Mole *couldn't* do what Alex did, but Mole, like me, preferred the short track. He "did his time" during the regular school day, and that's all he cared to do. And yet, who was the frequent flyer of after-school detentions? Go figure.

So far I was on Mole's good side, and I planned to keep it that way. Getting "what *I* deserved" meant Mole came through when I needed him. I remember frantically trying to finish up a school project, an electrified map of southern parts of Asia for social studies. It was a neat piece of handiwork with each country's capital city wired to blink with the push of a button. It needed another small light bulb. Mole brought me back the light bulb all right and a pocketful of spares as well. "Shopping the free market again, Mole?" I chuckled.

And then when I was about to fail my math course and needed coaching for an exam, Mole promised he would help (although he was failing more miserably than I was). "Hey, we get lucky sometimes with easy pickings," he said, handing me a copy of the exam. I didn't ask questions; I just smiled at the smug expression that told me once again Mole was there for me.

Like now. After a week in captivity, I was ready for some action.

"What do you say we head over to see if Cam's out of work yet?" I asked Mole.

He responded with his usual shrug.

"C'mon, man. I could go for some pizza," I added, heading to the door.

We walked the four blocks and entered the local convenience store where we could safely bet on finding Cam working for his dad. Broad-shouldered and wearing a blue work jacket, Cam was always easy to spot. I approached him at the checkout counter where he was waiting on some kid.

"Watch it, kid," I said. "That guy charges double and pockets the difference."

With eyes instantly widened, Cam shot a warning look at me. At the same time a graying head with a raised eyebrow rose from behind an opposite counter.

"Hey, Mr. Sullivan," I said cheerily, hoping Cam's father would see a connection between joking with the customer and turning a profit. But all he did was shuffle out to the back of his store with his bowed head shaking back and forth, probably praying for the souls of teenagers.

"Great timing, Tod," Cam said once the kid had left.

I hung my head and rapped my forehead with my clenched fist.

"Speaking of ripping people off," Cam said in a low voice while gesturing toward Mole, "can I trust *him* in here with anything that isn't nailed down?" Mole was standing with his back to us thumbing through magazines.

"Don't sweat it, Cam." I didn't bother to lower my voice. "Mole doesn't rip anyone off unless he's helping the needy."

"Yeah, that's what I mean. Like helping him *self*," Cam muttered.

Mole turned and shot a frown our way.

"What's your problem? You charge for looking?"

18

"Go ahead, Mole," Cam said with a look of disapproval meant for Mole and me. "Look all you want."

Mole crammed the magazine into its holder.

"Okaaay," I said, anxious to shift Cam's attention from Mole. "What do you say we pick up Darryl and head out for some pizza?"

Cam took a long look at me. "Have you *seen* Darryl in the last few days?" he asked.

"I've been in solitary for over a week. I haven't seen *anyone*, but never mind that now. What's up?"

"Well—and this is just between us—you too, Mole"—Mole was strolling over to join us—" 'cuz that's the way he wants it."

"Is Darryl all right?" I asked bracing myself for a nasty rerun.

"He was until his drunk excuse for an old man got a hold of him."

The words hit like a punch in the gut. I remembered too well what Darryl looked like the last time his father "got a hold of him."

"What did that creep do to Darryl this time?" Mole asked.

"Give me a few minutes to restock," said Cam.

The three of us restocked and were on our way.

Chapter Three

A FRIEND IN NEED

"The blue morons are at it again. Always sticking their noses where they don't belong," was Mole's response after Cam told us the police had questioned Darryl about some theft and vandalism at a local construction site. Darryl had been seen hanging around the site, and the cops had followed up on the lead.

"No way is Darryl into vandalism," I said.

"We know that, and that's what Darryl's father told them. Then the minute the cops were out of there, he let Darryl have it. Man, I mean *pounded* him."

Cam, Mole and I soon stood outside the chain link fence surrounding "the project," a partially completed block of apartments which was the town's new answer to the need for cheaper housing. Darryl's family had moved there a year ago when his dad couldn't hold down a job. I'd been inside their building only once while waiting for Darryl in the hallway. Curious to see the inside of his apartment, I'd stood in front of his door, but he had hastily closed it behind him as though anxious to seal off the inside from view. Darryl was not one to share much of his home life.

His apartment was on the second floor, and his bedroom window was within easy range of the pebbles we now lobbed to signal our arrival. He came to his window and gestured that he was on his way down.

We always figured Darryl was the good looking one in our group with his blue eyes, freckles, and bashful grin. Were it not for his shyness, I was sure the girls would have been all over him. Now as he approached us, I tried not to stare, but it was impossible to ignore the raw puffs of glossy skin that revealed only a sliver of his left eye.

Mole broke the silence as he let out a low whistle and recoiled from Darryl's face. "I sure hope you punched him out for that," he snarled.

Darryl shrugged.

We waited for him to speak, but he looked down and began dragging one foot back and forth along the dirt.

"Hey, I'll take care of him then," Mole continued as he jabbed with his clenched fists at a NO LOITERING sign. He punctuated his thrusts with "Pow! Pow!"

"Give it a break, Mole," Cam interrupted.

"That's all right, Cam," Darryl said in a soft voice. "He's not home now anyway. Hasn't been since last night. Just my Mom's home with my baby sister."

I'd never once heard Darryl refer to his father with scorn or hatred. Even now there was no sign of bitterness.

But there sure was for me. Standing next to the fence, Darryl reminded me of the first time I met him back in middle school when he was standing alone at a far corner of the school grounds with both hands stretched above his head gripping the fence links. At the same time he was scuffing the sand beneath him with his boot as though carving out an escape route. When I approached, he stopped and looked up for an instant without a word, then went back to his scuffing. To give him his space, I kept on walking.

For the next few days I watched for him. Most of the time he was sitting on the ground, leaning forward with one arm resting on his bent knees while poking a stick in the sand with the other.

Then one day, on one of our lunch breaks, I noticed him watching Mole and me play catch. Mole stopped mid throw to follow my attention.

"Weird guy, huh?—Get ready for this one, man," Mole said. He rifled the ball to smack it into my glove.

This time Mole and I continued our game of catch until class began. But the next time Darryl was watching us, I gestured a throw toward him as an invitation to join us. He nodded, then joined in our game with the extra glove I handed him. Mole hurled fast and furiously. Darryl did more than hold his own. In fact, he was a natural.

More of a natural than *I* was when it soon came time to play *Darryl's* game—a game he was forced to play with a very different set of rules. It was called "covering for his old man," and as I looked at the angry swelling on his face, I wondered once again, how the game would play out *this* time.

"Hey, want to grab a pizza with us?" I asked him.

"Not today, guys. I've—well—"

"Come on. It's no dark secret," chimed in Mole. "Everyone knows your old man is—"

"Shut up, Mole," Cam cut in.

"No sweat," I said to Darryl. "We'll see you here on Monday before school, O.K.?"

Darryl turned and headed back to the entrance of the project. Cam and I watched him until he disappeared through his doorway. Ahead of us, Mole nailed the NO LOITERING sign with a stream of spit, then signaled us to follow him outside the fence. We spent the rest of the afternoon at Franco's, staring at cold pizza.

Chapter Four

LET THE GAME BEGIN

On Monday morning Cam, Mole and I walked to
our usual stop outside the fence of Darryl's project.
The three of us lived within a couple of blocks of
each other, and if we took a half-mile detour,
Darryl's apartment was on our way to school. We
preferred the detour. It passed our favorite bakery
and led us through a littered alley separating
neglected buildings. Pitching pebbles through broken windows or tossing a breakfast handout to the
local trash picker did more to rev us up in the
mornings than hiking the main drags.

This morning was different. We waited longer than usual before Darryl appeared, then trudged along to school in awkward silence.

"Okay, guy," I finally said to Darryl. "What are you going to tell the idiots who ask what happened?" It wasn't so much the kids that bothered me. It was the adults. The ones who ask too many questions.

"Tell them you went golfing with Mole," Cam quipped.

"Yeah, and tell them his driving was smashing," I added.

All but Mole laughed. His eyes narrowed, and he gave us an icy stare.

"Fore," he called out as his clenched fist swung at our heads.

We reared back knowing that once again Mole's body language had the last word. A distorted smile settled on Darryl's swollen upper lip as he took in our antics.

"Darryl, anyone asks you why you look like that, tell 'em it was 'just a fight,' " I said. After all, it wouldn't be a normal day without some kind of commotion at the project.

Actually, Darryl hardly had to say a word during that school day. At least one of us was in each of Darryl's classes, and any time some kid as much as gave him a second look, we countered with a volley of excuses. In science he was suffering from a close encounter with formaldehyde; in history he was masquerading as a World War I casualty; in math he was further proof of the danger of getting too deep into *the numbers*. The cafeteria (a.k.a. the Hard Rock Café) had him caught in a meatball cross fire. In gym he'd been beaned by the wild one himself, four-eyed Maloney. Maloney's glasses were so thick he couldn't see the catcher, let alone the strike zone. On our way to English, the one class we were all in together, the four of us decided Darryl was simply to be allergic to Miss Buckley.

Chapter Five

INTO THE GATOR PIT

In our usual manner, Cam, Mole, Darryl and I
straggled into English precisely at the sound of the
late bell, then plopped ourselves like heavy sacks
into our seats. Mole and I sat at the front of the
class. Earlier in the school year he and I had sat
beside each other in our back row haven until the
day Boss Buckley nailed us for cheating and
promptly "advanced" us to the front row, each in
the opposite corner from the other. "How cheap is
that! Not even a flippin' second chance," Mole
objected, and he never quite forgave Miss Buckley

for that. He had been pinning his hopes for passing English on staying close enough to me to "share information" as he put it. Especially since it was widely rumored that her exams were coded and holed up at Fort Knox.

Instead of assuming the usual so-try-and-teach-me-something sprawl with our backs low in the seats and legs straight out in front, we sat upright, eyes widened, staring at Miss Buckley. She was wearing a boldly striped dress that blinked at us whenever she moved. She walked stiffly in an effort to hold in place her teetering hairpiece which was typically coming undone along with everyone's patience by the end of the school day. We figured that on any given day she must arrive home at least three inches shorter than when she left in the morning.

"What happened to *you?*" Miss Buckley asked Darryl, directing our attention from her deformed hairdo to Darryl's deformed face.

Darryl dropped his eyes, then stole a glance at me. "Just a fight," he said.

So much for class rules. "You oughta see what the other guy looks like," I blurted out.

"Yeah, kicked his butt right out of town," Mole added. "Never see that dude around here again."

I leaned forward to catch Mole's eye. He caught my drift. He glanced at the open textbook Miss Buckley was holding and raised his hand.

"William?"

"Ah, Miss Buckley, could we do something fun in here for a change? Like in biology. They get to cut up frogs in *that* class."

The stripes blinked. "Letting *you* cut up isn't what I have in mind," Miss Buckley retorted.

Mole grinned. "Look at it this way. I'd be getting under the frog's skin and not yours."

Laughter erupted while Miss Buckley's face briefly disappeared behind the pages of her book. We had her where we wanted her.

"How about showing a movie?" another voice chimed in from the back of the room. "Like Mr. Millsap does in history."

"Hey, any assemblies today?" someone else asked.

Miss Buckley's expression hardened, probably because she remembered the last assembly we'd gone to. It had featured a speaker on the Holocaust who had to explain to chatty Mole, practically in front of the whole school, that Mole was not the one hired to do the talking. Mole had been clueless. He'd been having too good a time amusing the girls sitting around him, who'd been too busy putting on their makeup to even realize there had been an interruption.

Today's interruptions continued. "Yeah, anything but English," a voice added.

"What do you mean 'anything but English'? You're doing English now," Miss Buckley broke in. "As long as you're communicating, you're doing English."

Her sigh told us she instantly regretted those words as Mole pressed on with renewed conviction.

"So why do we need to learn it if we're already doing it?" Mole persisted. "Why should I care what a 'participating' phrase is? I can talk. You know what I'm saying. I don't need none of this grammar stuff. I'm gonna be using my hands, and they won't be fixing sentences, I can tell you that."

"Yeah, you tell her," Cam said with a tone of sarcasm directed at Mole.

The stripes of Miss Buckley's dress sagged as she let out a deep sigh. Setting down her book, she picked up a stack of papers and held them up like a white flag of surrender.

"I'll say what I've said before," Miss Buckley went on, in a voice carefully controlled. "Communicating is two way. It involves *listening* as well as speaking. See if you can *hear* what I've said on your papers. *In siiiilence.*"

"*Lisssssssten* to the lady," Mole directed, looking back over his shoulder.

Miss Buckley narrowed her eyes at Mole, then blinked her way over to the door. She pointed at him, then at the doorway. "You! Out!"

"Just trying to help," Mole mumbled. He clipped his pen onto his jacket flap, then rose. Putting his hands in his pockets, he scuffed his way toward the door.

"Who are you staring at, four eyes?" Mole hissed at Hermie Hilton, the class genius sitting in the middle of the front row. Once past Miss Buckley, Mole raised a hand and showed the back of her head a short phrase in sign language, then disappeared.

Ignoring the round of snickers, Miss Buckley began to hand out our papers. She was interrupted by a knock at her door. The scowl on her face deepening, she blinked her way across the room again. Before she reached the door, Mr. Millsap opened it and held up some books he said he had come to swap. This wasn't the first time this had happened, and I had become convinced he was checking out more than books.

They stepped out into the hallway. Rising out of my chair and leaning toward the doorway, I gestured to the class to hush up.

"Welcome to my alligator pit," I heard Miss Buckley say with more than a whisper.

"A little more cold blooded than usual?" Mr. Millsap asked.

"What were my gator guys like in *your* class today?" she pressed on.

"Oh, whiny as usual—'A movie *again*?' "

"Hah!" Miss Buckley exclaimed like she'd hooked a big one. The door swung open, and I snapped back into my seat. Miss Buckley entered, armed with books and steeled to go on. As she breezed past me, I breezed back with a loud yawn.

"You going to leave enough oxygen for the rest of us?" she snapped.

I met her steely glare with one of my own. The reptiles' eyes stared at her from her "gator pit" as she walked down the aisles passing out papers to hands that snatched the pages like hungry jaws.

When I got mine, I shielded it from roving eyes. Then I sat, dismally staring at my D. A ten minute essay didn't cut it. Next time I'd see what I could pull together in fifteen.

Miss Buckley stood at the front of the classroom waiting for us to digest her comments in a silence broken by the crunch of my paper being rolled into a ball—then by another knock at the door.

"Tod, the door?" she asked impatiently.

I stood up slowly.

Opening the door, I found myself looking down into the face of a girl whose eyes darted uncertainly between me and the inside of the classroom.

"Is this Miss Buckley's English class?" she asked in a husky voice. She shifted her more than ample weight from foot to foot.

"Better known as 'the gator pit,' " I said quietly before Miss Buckley invited her in with an uncharacteristically pleasant voice.

The girl blushed and handed Miss Buckley a slip of paper. "I'm late because I went to the wrong class." Her voice quavered. I looked behind me at Darryl's grinning face, then away, to keep myself from cracking up.

"Oh, you don't want to stray far from *this* group," Miss Buckley replied with a wry smile. "Class, this is a new student, Louella Page." Louella cast her eyes to the floor. "Louella, you may sit in front of Darryl. The boy with the black eye."

The reptiles' eyes narrowed.

In her bunched up skirt covered with huge, faded flowers, Louella rustled past my row and down the aisle like a wilted shrub. Greasy strands of hair shielded her eyes and hung limply to her shoulders. Once she'd passed my seat, I caught a whiff of a musty odor like the one I get when scrounging through a week's worth of dirty laundry looking for a pair of socks. Darryl covered his nose. He'd caught a whiff too. I watched Louella sink into her chair and sit with her shoulders curled forward as though she still bore the weight of the book bag she had dropped at her feet.

I looked at Cam, who sat grinning, and at Darryl's bruised face now bulging more than ever in his effort to hold back his laughter.

That did it. I sat shuddering and snorting uncontrollably like a rapidly deflating balloon. Miss Buckley blinked her way to the door, then turned and pointed to me.

"Next!" With a grand sweep of her arm, she motioned for me to exit. Before leaving, I felt a sudden knot in my gut as I caught a glimpse of

Louella's reddened face and downcast eyes. A few minutes later, Mole, waiting in the office, loosened the knot with a grin and a thumbs-up sign. Then all tightened up again when I found myself looking into the grim eyes of the vice-principal, Mr. Peterson.

When ninth period dismissal finally ended another school day, Mole and I caught up to Cam and Darryl leaving the school grounds.

"Peterson give you a hard time?" Cam asked me.

"Naw, no problem. Just a detention is all. And old lady Buckley will probably drop my grade a few points. Next time is when they read the riot act, right, Mole? One more time in the office for you, and you may be out for good. It's be-nice-to-Buckley time for you, dude."

"So what," Mole said matter of factly. "I'm going to be out of here the day I turn sixteen anyway."

"That's when we might start learning something in English," Cam replied without disguising his irritation. "Amazing how different that class is when you guys aren't around."

"You won't be getting rid of me yet," Mole retorted.

"Good thing," Darryl said, raising an eyebrow. "You wouldn't want to miss a look at the new girl."

"A look?" Cam uttered with a snicker, "Or a sniff?"

Life was starting to feel normal again.

Chapter Six

ENTER THE CHAMELEON

On the day following Mole's one day suspension
from English class, the four of us entered Miss
Buckley's class well before the late bell. Mole
wanted to get there early. The essence of clothes
hamper hung in the room like an invisible fog. Mole
passed the row of desks where Louella had already
taken her place, then turned to us and rolled his
eyeballs. Next he looked at Miss Buckley who was
leaning over her desk, reading. Ignoring her end-of-
the-day hairdo, he told her how nice she looked.
Miss Buckley bolted upright as if someone had
pinched her from behind, then caught herself.

"Thank you, William," she said with cautious reserve.

After Mole asked if he might *please* open a window, he slid quietly into his seat and sat upright instead of in his usual slouch. If Miss Buckley was enjoying the transformation, she decided not to show it.

The class began with her asking for volunteers to read their "How To..." compositions. As usual, the first volunteer was Hermie Hilton whose topic was "How to Get the Bugs INTO Gourmet Cooking." While the rest of us moaned and gagged over images of sautéed grubs and baked stuffed moth wings, Mole sat quietly.

Finally, pressing the nozzles of imaginary cans of Raid while hissing through our teeth, several of us managed to eject Hermie from stage center. Mole seized the moment and brought a sudden silence to the room with a raised hand.

"Yes, William?" Miss Buckley said while probably wondering what stalling tactic he had in mind *this* time. Mole never volunteered for anything.

"I found that last reading rather sickening," Mole said. "I can give you all some relief. I'll get out my little Alka-Seltzer here."

Smiling in spite of herself, Miss Buckley nodded while Mole reached into his jacket pocket and pulled out a small square of tightly folded paper. He stood up, unfolded the paper, and stared at it for what seemed like forever. I knew he was trying to familiarize himself with my printout on "his" topic—"How To Cut Homework Time." Meanwhile, Darryl sat with his hands over his face, shuddering with silent laughter and thinking, I'm sure, about the homework time Mole had cut doing *this* assignment.

Mole began, "First you hire—just kidding!" In that instant he took my breath away and gained his audience.

He began again. "First you select a quiet study place." After a few fits and starts and mispronounced words, he was on his way.

Only as he approached the end could I relax enough to join in the chuckling of my classmates.

"And what's more," continued Mole, "be sure and keep your room neat so that when that long-range assignment you finished several days ago is due, you won't lose time looking for it. Besides, what teacher wants to correct a paper that's been hanging out with dirty laundry."

He grinned at Louella.

"And last but not least," Mole read on in a loftier tone, "if you don't understand your homework, don't get violent." Mole responded to the sniggering with a wry smile. "Copying homework that you've carved nasty words into is a sure waste of time. Taping ripped pages in your books is a bigger waste of time. And worst of all is having to spend your parents' money reordering a book you've tossed into a blazing fireplace. Take it from me. I know." (I thanked myself for remembering to say *parents'* money in Mole's case. After all, they never made him pay for anything.)

"Well—that's nice, William," Miss Buckley exclaimed as Mole lowered his paper and scanned his audience. Looking smugly over at me and then at

Darryl who was finally regaining his composure, Mole took his seat.

Not long after, Mole again brought the class to a dead silence by raising his hand. Miss Buckley had just asked what a *clause* is. "Well, you gotta have a subject and a whatchamacallit—a predicate," Mole said to the others' amazement, and mine, once I realized I couldn't see an open book or paper anywhere near him.

Next she asked if someone would tell her what a *subordinate clause* is. Before anyone could raise a hand, Mole had his up. "That's when you don't have a complete thought," Mole said casually. "*This from the most insubordinate kid in the whole school,*" I thought to myself. I couldn't resist giving him a little applause.

"Well, William, I'm impressed," Miss Buckley said as she wrote the definitions on the board.

"I lissten," Mole said, being careful not to use too many s's.

Toward the middle of class Miss Buckley asked Mole to deliver to the office the day's tally of kids who had cut her classes, an errand that up until then had been assigned only to her favorite few.

As Mole strutted out of the classroom, I noticed Louella smiling at him. By the time he returned, Louella had taken up where he had left off. Among other things she rattled off a pile of *prepositions*. Then, glancing over at Mole, she produced her own *appositive*—"William, a good English student."

Miss Buckley nodded in approval, then turned to the "good English student" who, I knew, was preparing himself for an about face.

"Well, William," Miss Buckley went on, unaware our chameleon was returning to his true colors, "do you think you can tell us what *interjections* are?"

Mole glared menacingly at Louella, then at Miss Buckley. "That's football talk," he said knowingly. "Quarterbacks get benched for too many of those." A few snickers encouraged the return of the Mole that his classmates knew best.

Miss Buckley's smile faded but quickly reappeared when she looked at Louella.

"Can you tell us, Louella?"

"An *interjection* is an exclamatory word," Louella answered, smiling at Mole.

"Like *Yuk!*" Mole muttered.

"Like *Wow!*" Miss Buckley exclaimed, smiling at Louella. "How about a *run-on*? Can anybody tell me what a *run-on* is?"

Mole raised his hand, then sprawled in his seat. "Yeah, everybody knows that," he said. "That's somebody who just keeps popping off at the mouth and doesn't know when to stop."

More laughter. Miss Buckley's jaw tensed, and she clasped her hands under her chin. "Louella, do *you* want to tell us what a *run-on* is?"

Louella came through.

Then, in one swift stroke, Mole went for the jugular. "I thought of *a positive* for you. Louella, a flaming—ah, forget it." Saved by the bell, Cam, Darryl, Mole and I, as always, were the first to charge out of the classroom and head to the exit.

Mole's strut began to irk me. "Just 'cuz you had a paper to hand in for a change didn't mean you had to read it," I said, not hiding my annoyance.

Mole's eyes narrowed. He pushed hard with the side of his body against the exit door which flung open and resounded off the railing. "Hey, I've stuck my neck out for you enough times. You owed me that paper, dude," he retorted.

"And I paid you what I owed. What is Buckley supposed to think when you can hardly read what *you* supposedly wrote?"

"What are you complaining about?" Mole replied. "Buckley liked it."

"Not as much as Louella liked *you*, huh, Mole?" Cam broke in.

"Butt out, Cam. Gimme a break. Louella could gag a maggot," Mole snapped.

"Easy, Mole," I said while giving a parting nod towards Cam as he turned onto the street he took to his father's store. "Look at it this way. You put on a good show. Louella thought you were the real deal. How was *she* to know? How about giving *her* a break?"

"Let's go bowling," Mole said.

For the sake of the pins, I prayed for gutter balls.

Chapter Seven

THE PIT DEEPENS

"*Now* do you want to give Louella a break?" Mole asked a few days later on our way home from school. We'd just sat through another one of those English classes that lately was slipping into a dull dialogue between Louella and Miss Buckley. Of course, it didn't help us that Louella actually *did* the homework *and* liked fancy words. Miss Buckley typically basked in Louella's offerings while the rest of us sat like gators stilled by a tropical heat. Louella seemed to enjoy the basking.

I pretended to shake out the static of a clinging dress while clutching with dismay a limp pine branch that mimicked a detached hairpiece. "How many novels did you say you've read, dear?"

"Oh, a plethora," Mole chirped, as he toyed with one of those far-out vocabulary words that only someone like Louella would wrap her head around.

"Isn't that wonderful, class. And the classics too," I replied. "This girl has no life, and we are so proud of her."

"I'm up to my greasy little scalp in books," Mole said, flicking away Louella's oily spikes with a neck-wrenching toss of his head.

Mole, Darryl, and I seriously considered sending Louella some poisoned Milk Duds. We settled on slipping one of Mole's old horror comic books featuring *The Bride of Alligator Swamp* into her book bag the following day instead. The cover presented a gathering of toothy gators. Each had an outstretched neck poised for a grab, and each eyed the water's edge where a scaly hag, veiled in a mist of swamp gas, was lurking.

Mole, always one for the personal touch, had smeared red letters dripping from the gators' mouths that read, *"We want you, Louella,—'til death do us part."*

When she found the comic book, I heard Louella's gasp. I turned and watched her slowly remove it with her fingertips, as though pulling it from swamp water. She dropped it into Miss Buckley's wastebasket.

Cam, Mole, Darryl and I dutifully sat with our eyes fixed on the poem of the hour, "The Road Not Taken." Miss Buckley, probably anxious to preserve the ninth period calm, said nothing.

With the patience of predators, we lay in wait for a few days. The time for our next move came on one of those composition days in English when Miss Buckley asked Louella to read her theme on "The Value of Cooperation." She read of "two friends whose inspiring attributes I shall never consign to oblivion." Putting my head on my desk, I faked illness. Okay, so her writing stunk too, and I didn't care if she knew it. Then again, maybe she had a ghost writer because she couldn't possibly have *one* friend let alone two.

Catching Darryl's eyes, I pointed at Louella's book bag resting near his foot. As Miss Buckley translated into English Louella's deep wisdom that yes, cooperation *is* a virtue we could all benefit from, cooperative footwork began to move Louella's bag down the aisle. It moved to the back of the room, then across it, spilling most of its contents along the way. Finally it lay flattened in the back corner like roadkill.

When the bell rang, Miss Buckley, used to our bolting to the exits, disappeared into the crowded hallway. Meanwhile, Louella, searching around her desk, found only her ragged *Thesaurus.* With amusement we watched her bob around the classroom gathering assorted books and papers that plotted her bag's course. Most wore the stamp of disapproval from dirty sneaker treads. We snickered as she got down on all fours to crawl and stretch out her arms beneath the desks. That's when we heard it.

First, in her crouched position, I thought it was the click of a bone. But when I saw and heard the ripping of her shoulder seam, I realized buttons had just been fired from her tight-fitting shirt. Mole grinned. To two girls who had lagged behind, this now became a call for action. They helped Louella gather her belongings, then quickly fled the classroom.

Louella stood, her hand gripping her clothing above her waist. Cam stepped forward and handed Louella her bag which he had picked off the floor. "Let's go, guys," he said and headed out the door. I started to follow, but Mole's steely eyes nailed me in place.

"Can't leave a *dam*sel in distress," Mole hissed. Louella's eyes fastened on the bag, then at Mole, who stood smirking nearby. Throwing insults definitely wasn't her strong suit because the best she could do at that moment was to call Mole a *dirtball* which only sent more jeers her way.

Mole went to the doorway and looked down the hallway, then turned to face us. "Did you get all your *trash*?" he asked Louella as he braced his body rigidly between the sides of the doorway. The few of us remaining in the classroom clustered around the doorway, further barring her exit.

With tears welling in her eyes, Louella let out a brief yelp like an injured puppy. Except for Mole, the blockade broke up. Mole remained in the doorway leaning against the side with one leg stretched across.

"School day's over," I said to Mole impatiently.

Mole lowered his leg but couldn't resist the impulse to raise it slightly as Louella passed through. We chuckled as she teetered and hastened from the room with a whiny grunt, straight into some oncoming students. With another whiny grunt she disappeared down the hallway.

Mole held out his hand to me. "Put it there," he said. I did.

For the rest of that afternoon Mole and I pumped iron at the local 'Y'. With every lift Mole grunted, "She's dead meat."

"Easy, Mole. How about another ten pounds."

"Dead meat," he panted.

Chapter Eight

SLAM POETRY

By now one would think our game was finished and
we'd be ready to move beyond the world of taunting
Louella in English class. But it was fun—a needed
distraction in the last period of a long school day.
And she was such an easy target! An inviting
target! Hey, in our minds she might as well have
worn a bull's-eye on her shirt, and every direct hit
would have been deserved. In fact, all considered,
we had been downright merciful. Pretty harmless
stuff, really. And what's more, we'd been subtle
enough not to get caught in the act.

Actually, we might have moved on had it not been for the inspiration of poetry.

Miss Buckley was in the habit of asking Louella to read because Louella *liked* to read. She stood up and read ancient odes like they'd never gone out of style, her book bag safe between her ankles. And it seemed that she was chosen because she outranked us all, and yes, to those who sat near her and didn't have a blocked up nose, in one way she *did*. When Miss Buckley asked us to sharpen our senses for some in-class poetry writing, mine were already honed like razors.

When I was done with my ode, I couldn't resist passing it to Mole. When he got it, he cracked up.

"You care to share the good times with the rest of us so we can all have a laugh?" Miss Buckley asked him. She was always eager to share students' writing. (Mistake #1)

Mole leaned forward in his seat and craned his neck to see me past the faces of the front row. "Hey, good rhythm, Tod," he said. "Rhyming isn't bad either."

Then, after turning to face the class, he announced, "You all should hear this."

"Miss Buckley won't like it," I replied anxiously and turned to face the front of the classroom with my hands cupped in front of my eyes. A prickly warmth spread over my upper body.

"I'll be the judge of that," said Miss Buckley. "William, since Tod is being so modest, *you* read it."

(Mistake #2—mine!) In an instant I could have swooped in on Mole to seize and destroy my reckless rhyme. Instead, while Mole hesitated, I sat, hoping to morph into a floor tile.

Then, all too suddenly, the class took up Miss Buckley's cause and chanted, "Read it! Read it!" Mole, not one to disappoint his fans, promptly stood up to face them.

"An Ode to Louella," he read loud and clear. Miss Buckley's smile faded.

"An *ode,* Miss Buckley," Mole said to reassure her. The class was eager for Mole to continue. With my heart pounding, I took a deep breath and sat still. Mole cleared his throat.

"I know a young girl named Louella
Her knowledge of English marvella
The rest of us could
In English do good
Without a Louella to smella.
        P.S. Is there anyone here who will tella?"

A new wave of warmth spread on my face and neck as I looked straight ahead. Then Louella darted past me and out the door. An unbearable silence seized the classroom. I could feel the eyes boring into me. The heat turned up again. This time full blast. I stared at my desk top.

"So, Tod, this is *your* creation!" Miss Buckley confirmed as she snatched the ode from Mole like the mother of all ravenous reptiles.

"He didn't want to—" Mole started in.

"I'm speaking to Tod," she interrupted.

"It's only a rough draft," I replied in an effort to quell my flood of embarrassment. The room remained quiet.

"It's a rough, cheap shot is what it is. Something Mr. Peterson will take up with you."

"Whatever happened to freedom of speech?" Mole piped in.

Without missing a beat, Miss Buckley began:

"There once was a piece of work,
And some folks would call him a —"

"Hey, you can't say that," Mole cut in.

With a satisfied humph, Miss Buckley handed me my limerick, my one-way ticket to Peterson's den of repenters, and gestured to the door. I strode out into the hallway, glad to be away from the suffocating heat of the classroom.

On the way to Mr. Peterson's office I felt the urge to tear the poem to bits and toss them into an open locker. Instead I folded it and put it in my pocket.

I watched Mr. Peterson scan the lines. When his eyes looked up, I knew he wanted to stun me with his infamous hawk-like gaze, but all I really saw was a tortured Louella fleeing from the classroom.

I silently added one more line to my ode—

"You're about to get yours, young fella."

Chapter Nine

JAWING ON THE HOME FRONT

That afternoon I headed straight home from Mr. Peterson's office instead of meeting up with my friends.

"Home early for a change!" my mother greeted me.

"Big test I have to study for," I lied, grabbing a Dr. Pepper and a bag of Doritos from the kitchen before hurrying to my room. I dropped my books to the floor and tossed the chips on my desk, wondering why I'd grabbed them when I wasn't hungry. As I was about to put on my headphones, Mole and Darryl came into my room. I signaled for them to shut the door.

Mole propped himself on the edge of my desk. "Have you told your mother about your school day?" he asked, opening the bag of chips and cramming a handful in his mouth.

"Of course not, and I don't plan to. I got a week of detentions starting Monday, you know. Here, Darryl, have some chips," I said, handing him the bag. It was easy to forget he was in the room at times.

"Buckley and Peterson are idiots," Mole pressed on. "You were telling it like it is. Louella deserved it."

"Duh, earth to Mole! You could have pleaded the fifth for me and not read that thing, or you could have stopped short of the punch line. But no, in Mole mode, you had to deliver the punch. And just so there's no confusion, *we're* the dirtballs, *you're* the idiot, and I could be dead meat," I said. Mole winced. He wasn't used to my being so brutally honest.

"If you had *my* dad running the show, you wouldn't be dead meat," Mole countered. "Like Ma always says, 'Dad will take care of it.' He'd tell Old Buckley she shouldn't be wasting our time with poetry, that boys will be boys, that we didn't *hurt* anybody, that we're basically good kids who are cheated by schools that don't motivate us enough. Remember when I was picked up for throwing rocks at the windows of a parked truck? By the time my dad got done hammering the guy, the dumb driver was apologizing to *us* for parking where he did. My dad would have had Buckley begging us to forgive her for making me read your poem—and for calling you a jerk."

"*Almost* calling," I corrected, believing Miss Buckley would never have actually said it. "I guess you got all the luck, Mole. My parents can't even come up with excuses for me."

I heaved a deep breath. I was tired and reached for my headset to make it obvious I wanted to be alone for a change.

"See you later, Tod. I guess you won't miss these," Mole said, grabbing the Doritos.

"Sure, Mole. Give some to Darryl."

They left, and now it was just The Demons, but on a day that was positively the pits, not even they could offer relief.

Chapter Ten

A CHILI EVENING

My parents were masters of timing. I was finally wrapping up my week of "secret" detentions and on my way to freedom when it suddenly hit the fan. To guarantee a case of indigestion, they waited until I polished off my fourth bowl of chili. Then they sent the evening completely down the tubes with the appearance of an opened stamped envelope and the written notice it contained.

"In—danger—of—failing—English"

My father read the words in a voice I had never heard him use before—very slowly and distinctly—

as though English was so foreign to me that I might fail to recognize it if he spoke it any faster.

I picked up my spoon and began rolling it briskly between my fingers. "Yeah, Dad, Buckley's a poor excuse for a teacher."

"Miss B? She was a good teacher when *I* had her," Tracey chimed in as she scraped up melted remains of peach ambrosia ice cream. "A lot of kids liked her."

"No one asked you," I shot back.

"Removal—from—classroom—has—lowered—his—average," my father read on.

Tracey refilled her bowl and began chowing down more mounds of ice cream.

"Yeah, I was sent out," I retorted. "And I hadn't said a word. I was Miss Buckley's patsy. It was a cheap shot." I looked over at Tracey. "I thought you didn't *eat* desserts."

"Dishonesty—has—affected—grade," my father droned on. I gripped my spoon tightly. My parents met each other's eyes across the table as my sister continued to savor every spoonful.

"Huh? What the? See what I mean about cheap shots? I don't know what she's talking about."

My parents suddenly looked like they'd been hit with their own cases of indigestion.

Tracey responded with louder bowl scraping— then the clatter of dishes as she loaded them into the dishwasher. My spoon slid from my sweaty fingers.

"Does *she* have to be here?" I asked, glaring at Tracey.

"It sounds like I should meet this poor excuse of a teacher who takes cheap shots," my mother said, ignoring my question.

"Yeah, and all she would tell you is that we put a comic book in this new girl's book bag to see if we could get a smile out of her—she's pretty sad."

The eyes were not convinced.

"And about the poem we wrote sort of teasing her about how good she is in English. Yeah, that's where the dishonesty rap comes in," I said, grasping at straws.

"How's that?" Dad asked.

"You know. Saying she's good in English when she really isn't. The stuff she writes is awful."

"Well," Dad went on, "Miss Buckley *did* mention your poetic license running amuck. *And* something about your doing someone's assignment for him."

"Where does she say that?" I said, standing up and reaching for the slip of paper.

"Oh, you won't find it here," Dad replied. "I've already spoken with Miss Buckley. She seems nice enough on the phone. She told me a little about your friend William. *He's* not so nice."

"You mean that Mole kid who shows up at our doorstep?" Tracey asked, beginning to wipe down the counters. "My friends can't believe that Tod hangs out with him."

"Mom!" I protested.

"So what about this assignment that you did for him?" my father pressed on.

I didn't answer.

"I have the incriminating draft you didn't delete, Tod," he said.

My mouth filled with the sharp taste of chili.

"Well, tell you what, Mister Poet," Dad continued. "I guess what we have to do for this sorry cast of characters you've had the misfortune to be thrown in with is to show them what a good English student really is. Like what you used to be. And your chances of being a good English student are better if you're not hanging around places like pizza parlors and bowling alleys. And your chances of that are better without money to spend. We'll cancel your allowance for awhile, until you earn some solid credit. Get my drift?"

"But, Dad," I protested.

"No buts. You're digging that hole we've talked about, Tod. It's getting so deep I don't recognize you, pal. I can dangle some rope for you, but it's *your* job to grab it and pull yourself up."

For a moment I sat stunned. He might as well have dangled a line of barbed wire. I slid my chair back taking care to scrape its legs loudly against the floor. I stood up and shoved it into the table. Leaving the kitchen, I heard my mother cheerfully exclaim, "Oh, look! The kitchen is cleaned up, and I didn't have to lift a finger!" That wasn't the effect that I had hoped for.

Chapter Eleven

ROPE CLIMBING

I was certain now that if the adults I knew were asked to list their worst peeves, I would have shown up somewhere between backed-up plumbing and carpenter ants. Again I was grounded; this time I had to raise my English grade and demonstrate good behavior before my parents would commute my sentence. My preparation for parole began with a room fix.

First I rescued my desk chair, floored by a daily drop of clothing flung over its back. Next, I upended my desk to clear its top of empty soda cans, food wrappers, and the crisp remains of a science bug collection I had handpicked from our overhead light fixtures. Then, sitting with one leg swinging to the rhythm of music, I boarded Odysseus' ship and set sail, feeling the pull of the changing tide. Before long the music was muted, and the pages were turning. For me, a new era in English was beginning.

My momentum only increased. Miss Buckley, never shying away from failure, soon returned to poetry. She had us each adopt a poem, one we could choose ourselves and then present to the class. I hunted through the collection of Ogden Nash with the goal of finding a poem that would make the class laugh. Miss Buckley said I did better than that. With Nash's "Seeing Eye to Eye is Believing," I made the class *think*. Progress was coming more easily than I would have thought.

Soon two events happened that clinched my success in English. It began with the loss and gain of Louella. First we noticed what we were no longer noticing. Dark, nondescript pants were replacing faded flowered skirts. Even better, sitting near

Louella no longer meant you had to pay through the nose. But we also noticed she no longer volunteered in class. Instead, with her eyes shielded behind her hand cupped to her forehead, she had become quiet and dispirited. Then she stopped coming to class at all. Although we all were wondering why, only Mole couldn't resist inquiring about "smella Ella." That's when Miss Buckley informed us that Louella was in one of her earlier classes, one that we later found out was "one of those smart classes." I felt an inner relief. The Louella chapter of my life was over.

As Louella moved up and out of the pit, Mole spiraled further down into his own, and that was the second event. Busted for our cheating fiasco and put at the very end of his administrative rope, he was being careful. We thought there was hope for the problem child. That is, until *he* thought he had met another pushover.

I'm sure in his mind the fault lay with the full moon and the low-grade meat that was being served in the school cafeteria that day, but without a doubt, several of us, including an ever growing number of "Mole scorners," witnessed him stabbing a chunk of food and catapulting it off the end of his fork. Unfortunately for him, a substitute teacher witnessed it too. Though small in build, the teacher came up from behind and rested a heavy hand on Mole's shoulder just as Mole was preparing to reload. Mole wheeled around in his seat. People like Mole don't do well with surprises. Especially physical surprises. People like teachers don't do well with verbal abuse. Especially abuse directed at them.

"What's your name, young man?" the substitute asked sternly.

Mole looked at him with cold narrow eyes.

"Dumb-ass!" he hissed.

"Is that your first or your last?"

Chapter Twelve

ONE GOOD TURN?

"You miss me?" Mole asked Cam, Darryl, and me one afternoon as he suddenly appeared from across the street and joined us on our way home from school. We hadn't seen Mole since his expulsion, and it was rumored he was working odd jobs at his dad's small engine repair shop, including his specialty, lawn mower tune-ups. I knew he'd be good at it. Mole could be surrounded with engine parts of a friend's ATV *one* minute, only to have it up and running the next.

"I'll tell you, Mole. Our class will never be the same without you," I said, trying to sound regretful while at the same time thinking about my grades and my home status continuing to improve in his absence. I was now somewhere up with squeaky doors on the list of adult peeves. "What's up with you?"

"Ah, still working out, but it ain't at 'the Y'. Ever try doing lawn mower lifts all day?—Hey, anyone for Franco's? I'm starved."

"Sorry. Can't today," I said. "I'm working now with Cam at his dad's store."

Mole's posture stiffened.

Having earlier shared with Cam the details of my money shortage, I had my problem solved. Cam had talked his father into offering me a job at his convenience store—cleaning up the place and helping him deliver bags of groceries to customers who lived nearby—elderly shut-ins and other ailing folks who couldn't get out and do their own shopping. It was only for a few afternoon hours a week, and a half day on the weekends, but that's all I needed. My parents didn't object. The only opposition came from Mole.

"Your parents got plenty of money. Why do *you* need to work?"

I didn't answer him.

"Hey, my brother is getting his own car next week. Cruisin' time, man."

"You've got Darryl to go with you, you know," I said.

Mole frowned at me and continued walking with Darryl while Cam and I headed in a different direction to the store where Mr. Sullivan was waiting.

I didn't share Mole's disappointment. Not yet.

Chapter Thirteen

A TASTE OF KINDNESS

Not until I met Miss Tippett, or Tippy as Cam and I liked to call her, did I start sharing Mole's disappointment. To get to her place, Mr. Sullivan and I pulled up on a street lined with hulking triple decker houses. Whoever built these multi-family units figured he had a good thing. They were all alike—flat-roofed and sided with shingles made to resemble bricks. Each building had a triple stack of wrap-around porches. Once we pulled up to the curb, I had special instructions from Mr. Sullivan to both bring in Miss Tippett's groceries and put them away for her.

With lagging steps I walked around to the back of the van and pulled out the last two bags of groceries. "She lives on the first floor, Tod," he said when I stopped by his front window. "She's very frail so don't let her lift anything. After this one, you're through for the day. Take a taxi home with this if you need to." He handed me a ten and drove off.

I climbed the bowed steps of Tippy's flat and stood facing a line of wet, stained laundry that looked like it had been hauled fresh from the Ganges River. Lowering my head, I stepped cautiously around spaces worn through by rotting planks on the porch floor. At the same time I tried to dodge the damp sleeves and thick brown stockings that licked at my head and shoulders. Once through this obstacle course, I stood in front of an open screen door that creaked on its side hinges. I anchored the door with my foot to avoid being snagged by the frayed wire edges of its torn mesh, then pressed a rusted doorbell button. After a few moments I thumped hard on the inside door several times with my fist while balancing the groceries with my raised knee.

"Coming, coming," a gravelly voice called from the inside. "I'm not deaf, you know." There was a rattling of latches, and then the inside door opened slightly. A woman's face, a road map done in relief, peered out from behind it, first with a cautious look at me, then with recognition at the bags I was about to drop. She released a chain lock and opened the inside door.

"Come in, Sonny," she said, holding the screen door open with shaking curled hands. I stepped in to near darkness.

After she relocked the door, I followed her halting legs down a narrow hallway into a small kitchen, wishing I could pitch her forward with some of that energy that rocked her sideways.

"Use the counter here, Sonny," she said. I plopped the bags down.

"My name's Tod. Tod Whitney," I said, stretching my arms and shoulders and taking a deep breath of well-used cat box. I tried not to wrinkle my nose.

"OK if I pat him?" I asked as I began to reach down to a gray cat curled up beside the radiator in the corner of the kitchen.

"Oh, sure. My Dustball's old like me. Not going anywhere."

I stroked the gray fur while Miss Tippett opened the doors of her only two cabinets.

"Mr. Sullivan asked me to help you put your groceries away," I said.

"Go ahead, Sonny. He's worried that my shaky hands will drop things," she said with her shaky voice.

I stood up and began unloading groceries. Her cabinets were empty except for torn and stained shelf paper held in place by a few cans and a couple of old yellowed boxes lying on their sides. I peered inside to make sure nothing was alive before reaching in to add some fresh cans and boxes. One whiff in the refrigerator, however, and I knew I'd be hauling out the dead. I changed the temperature settings, then tossed out soured milk, moldy lemons, a slimy cucumber, and anything else offensive to eyes, nose and touch. Then I stocked the shelves with dairy products, fresh produce, and several frozen chicken pies.

After checking the bags to be sure they were empty, Miss Tippett scuffed over to a tin sitting on her tabletop. She pried off its lid and held the tin under my face. I inhaled the sweet smell of molasses cookies.

"How about some of these?" she asked, the wrinkles of her face deepening with pleasure.

I thought of the yellowed boxes and the sour milk.

"Ah, no thanks," I replied, pulling the bill out of my pocket and glancing at my watch.

"They're homemade," her gravelly voice pleaded. I looked at the shaking tin and at the sad old red-rimmed eyes. I reached in and popped a cookie into my mouth. She smiled and held the tin near my face again. I took two more.

"They *are* good. Thanks. I've got to head back now."

"Would you like a ginger ale?" she asked, pointing to a dusty six-pack on the floor.

"No thanks. I'm a Dr. Pepper guy." Then, to hasten my exit, I added, "Gotta be back at the store by five," I lied. "Those cookies really *are* good." She tucked a couple in my jacket pocket.

I followed her slow steps to the front door and waited for her to unbolt the locks. When I stepped out onto her porch and through the laundry, eager to be on my way, my view into a yard diagonally across the street brought me to a halt.

"What is it?" she asked as I stepped back to the doorway, parting the laundry so she could see across the street.

"That girl with the little kid. Does she live there?"

"Louella? Oh, yes, she moved in weeks ago. Do you know her?"

"A little," I said, staring at the yard and watching the kid laugh and throw his arms around Louella's neck. "I mean—I hardly know her at all, really."

"She's my guardian angel," Miss Tippett replied.

"Oh yeah?" I drew a deep breath while imagining Mole's laughter. "I gotta be going now," I said and headed towards the steps.

"Thanks, Sonny. Will you be coming back?" she called after me.

"Ah, that's up to you and Mr. Sullivan. Thanks for the cookies."

"You can thank Louella for those. She's the one who made them. Bye now."

The locks sliding into place echoed the stirrings in my stomach. After one quick glance at the building across the way, I jumped from the porch to the ground below, feeling a sickness as I landed. I put my hand over my mouth and hastened around the corner making it just in time; for there, behind a screen of bushes, I stopped, bent over at the waist, and splattered Louella's cookies onto the dirt beneath me.

Chapter Fourteen

THE MOLE EFFECT

Mole's idea of cruising was looking better all the time, but making money still had the edge. I was back at the store the following day, giving Cam the Louella-scoop. "If I could do it," I told him, "I'd stay in the store and clean out the dairy case and wash windows all day. What are the chances of that?"

"Not good."

"How about delivering to everyone on the list *except* for Tippy?"

"Not good either. With a little luck," Cam reasoned, "you won't see Louella at all. And at worst, you might. A bummer, but you can live with it."

For several weeks the "little luck" was with me. I was enough of a regular at Miss Tippett's that I could anticipate most of the store supplies she needed, and enough of a regular that I was Sonny half the time and Tod the other. And during those visits I didn't see Louella. I was lulled into thinking that the one time I *had* seen her was pure rare coincidence.

But there was a piece of both Cam and me that was curious about Louella, and the day came when I began to satisfy our curiosity.

It was one of those raw drizzly spring days that covered everything in a gray mist. As Mr. Sullivan and I pulled up to the curb, I looked over at Louella's yard, empty as I had expected it to be. All was quiet in the neighborhood except for the sound of my footsteps in the road's layer of wet sand and the metallic thud of the van doors after I removed Miss Tippett's groceries. Then the hum of the van pulling away was suddenly drowned out by the persistent crying of a child that came from the direction of Louella's house.

I climbed Miss Tippett's steps. I didn't have to knock anymore. No sooner did I arrive at the door when the old reddened eyes appeared from behind it. They brightened as I entered.

"Back again," I said, answering her smile.

A drab overcoat thrown over her shoulders covered all but the front of Miss Tippett's wine colored dress where gray cat fur clung like a fine mesh. The house felt cold and damp and still smelled of cat box.

I followed her down the hallway, walking to the slow tapping of the cane she held in both hands and to the sound of labored breathing that hissed like a bicycle pump. This time I didn't feel the urge to pitch her forward.

"It's the dampness," she said as we entered the dark kitchen. "My joints aren't behaving today—for the same reason that back door over there won't close." She pointed with her cane to a door hung up on the outside of its threshold.

I went over and gave the handle a firm lift upward, then tugged and scraped the door along the wood beneath it until it latched, blocking out the bone-chilling air and the sound of the crying child.

"There," I said. "Project done." She began pouring out so many thanks and praises that I felt like telling her my name was Tod—not God.

"How can you stand listening to that screaming kid?" I asked, anxious to change the subject.

The sudden solemn look in Miss Tippett's eyes told me I had just fallen from grace. Tempted to put her head of lettuce firmly between my teeth and leave it there, I began quickly tossing groceries from the bags into her cabinets and refrigerator.

"Shame on you," she started in with as much sternness as her gravelly voice could muster. "That child has had a host of ailments, and every time we hear him cry, we are thankful that he has the strength to do it. If you only knew! No father! A mother we seldom see! Louella takes care of that child every single afternoon."

I finished unloading the groceries in silence, then bent down to pat Dustball. That's when we heard the gentle tapping on the front door. I listened while Miss Tippett shuffled down the hallway and opened the door. "Come in, dear," she said in a voice ringing with sweetness.

"Hi, Miss Tippett," an all too familiar voice answered. "I hope you're better. I have the medicine you want."

"Oh, aren't you wonderful, dear. Come into the kitchen, Ben. Dustball's waiting for you."

At that moment I was seized by what I would later call *the Mole effect.* Suddenly Mole, who had never heard of Miss Tippett and never would if I had my way, was *with* me, prodding me to do something dramatic and startling. "*Yeah, put the grocery bag over your head. You don't have to tell Louella it's so YOU can't see HER.*" Or "*Sprint out the back door. Later tell the old lady that you suddenly needed a good dose of fresh air.*" Or "*Hang in tough. Threaten Louella with a drug bust.*"

Then Mole's voice disappeared as I met Louella's startled face and the puffy damp eyes of what I guessed to be a three or four year old.

"Hi, Louella," I said in a voice squeaking with embarrassment.

Louella stopped and abruptly turned to Miss Tippett. "I'm sorry. I didn't know you had company. Ben and I can come back later," Louella said.

Before Miss Tippett could answer, I said, "It's O.K., Louella." I continued patting the cat, more in the interest of soothing *myself* than Dustball. "Don't mind me." I turned and knelt down to the boy who was still sniffling and tear-smudged.

"Who's *this* little guy?" I asked.

"That's my brother Ben. Say 'Hi,' Ben."

Ben clutched Louella's legs and buried his head without responding. Louella scooped up the child and headed out of the kitchen. Miss Tippett started to follow.

"I'll get the door, Miss Tippett," I said.

Hoisting Ben every few seconds, Louella walked down the porch steps and headed home.

Mole's voice intruded again. "*I'll get the door, Miss Tippett,*" he mimicked. "*Let me know when I should start playing the violins, Tod.*"

Chapter Fifteen

BYGONES

Maybe it was those bloodhound eyes that always greeted me at the door. Maybe it was that grin each time I discovered a can of Dr. Pepper that Mr. Sullivan had packed with her groceries at her request. For whatever reasons, in spite of Mole's scornful laughs which flashed in my head at times, I had taken it upon myself to do a few repairs for Miss Tippett on my *own* time. They were easy ones like sanding down and staining the back threshold, and, with my father's help, replacing some of her porch planks so they could safely hold her rocking chair. To her, the completion of each task was like the completion of the eighth wonder of the world.

After I countered her praises with "Oh, no big deal," she would toddle over to an old carton and fish out some little gift she could repay me with. Because she was so insistent, I stopped trying to refuse her presents. I ended up with stuff like an old ticket stub from the first show to open in the local Princess Theater, and a pair of eyeglasses worn by a great-great-grandfather Tippett who was the only Tippett, she said, to bring fame to the family name. "Too bad the old cuss did it through horse thieving." Of all the gifts, she was proudest of a paperweight with its brightly colored coral reef. I thought of Aunt Lucy. I wrapped it in paper towels and tucked it in my pocket.

On one of my workdays at the store, Mr. Sullivan informed me that Miss Tippett had called and needed me at her place, with no explanation. I could walk there in about fifteen minutes. Sprinting through the alleyways on that day, I made it under ten.

When I turned the corner onto her street, I spotted Louella sitting on Miss Tippett's steps holding Ben at her side while Miss Tippett rocked on her porch behind her. The old woman's hands were clasped in her lap. As I approached, I noticed her eyes staring straight ahead, vacant and disregarding, not at all like the eyes that normally greeted me. I stood at the base of her steps, greeting her with an uncertain wave and "hello." There was no response.

Ben squeezed in closer to Louella as I climbed the steps. He then lowered his head onto her lap as Louella greeted my wave with a barely audible, "Hi, Tod." She stroked Ben's thin, pale face.

Miss Tippett continued to rock and stare emptily. A roughly folded newspaper lay on the porch floor beside her.

I caught Louella's eyes, and she lowered them to the newspaper. The corner of the paper fluttered as I moved toward it. Catching sight of long gray fur, I lifted the pages far enough to reveal the lifeless form of Dustball lying on his side.

"Miss Tippett would like you to bury Dustball," Louella said in a hushed tone.

I stared at the cat, then at Miss Tippett in her hypnotic state. "I'll need a shovel," I said, trying to keep my voice steady.

Louella lifted Ben's head, then stood and held his hands to raise him up on his feet. "We have some in our shed," she said.

She and Ben led me around to the back of her house where she opened a rotting shed door behind which lay a jumble of assorted rusted tools and flower pots. Louella and I each took a shovel.

The afternoon was quiet except for the steady scraping of shovel tips against the hard packed earth and buried rocks. We dug a deep hole and gently lowered Dustball into his grave; then the two of us took turns tossing shovelfuls of dirt and tamping the earth until the hole was filled. Ben found a flat rock and set it down to mark our burial place.

Whether it was from the dust of our digging, the sight of the dead cat, the eerie trance of Miss

Tippett, or something else entirely, we didn't know; but suddenly Ben was in the grip of an attack that threw his chest into violent spasms of coughing and wheezing. After, he lay weak and wilted on Miss Tippett's porch floor.

Then the smell of Ben's messed pants sent Louella scrambling to pick him up and whisk him away. "Sorry," she said softly as she lifted his limp form.

"No need to apologize to me," I said catching her eye. "My nose has never been very reliable anyway."

I followed Louella home hauling the shovels while she carried the spent child into her house. I leaned the tools against the inside shed wall, then wrestled the outside latch into place. There was no padlock or key, and no need for either. No robber would put *this* neighborhood on his hit list. So much was losing its grip. Peeling paint. Broken shingles. Warped wood crumbling from rot. Screens curling around the edges of gaping holes. This had to be life on the edge.

Up until now, the only "living on the edge" I knew of was when Mole, a couple years back, became the poster boy for stupidity. He ignored posted warnings and jumped onto his cousin's jet ski only to be tossed soon after into swollen flood waters. Four overworked firemen risked their lives to rescue him, and Mole viewed the ordeal as his personal badge of honor. "I'm front page material," he announced proudly.

No, here I figured people quietly existed hand to mouth.

I stood outside Louella's front door until she returned. Ben was inside, asleep. Louella and I sat on her front steps and watched Miss Tippett's steady rocking from across the street. While tears began to stream down our faces unashamedly, Mole's violins could have screeched to the heavens for all I cared.

The Mole effect, I realized, had died with Dustball.

Chapter Sixteen

WILD RIDES, FRIED DOUGH AND SIDESHOWS

Come early May, each day I celebrated the kitten that Louella and I presented to Miss Tippett, who was quickly returning to her normal self thanks to pet therapy. Cisco, named by Miss Tippett after an old TV cowboy, was a hit!

Louella and I had discovered Cisco thanks to a sign advertising Free Kittens at a home near the center of town. The cat wasn't the only discovery though. Ben, we now realized, liked my company. He was eager to join Louella and me on our walk to the "kitten place," and he clutched my hand all the way. When Louella and I promised that the kitten would be *his* pick, Ben and I became best buds. And not just for the moment. Louella told me, soon after, that Ben now watched and listened for Mr. Sullivan's van. I knew then that Louella and Ben's sudden appearances during my visits to Miss Tippett didn't "just happen," and I found myself watching for them too.

Nowadays it was easy to jack up the moods at Miss Tippett's. When Louella and Ben arrived, all I needed were a couple of ping pong balls. Cisco, a jock, quickly drew Ben into the action. With leaps, grabs, and Ben's shrieks of laughter, Ben and the cat played to the gallery. We all answered with cheers and rounds of high fives.

I chuckled on those days when Miss Tippett called in to the store with a list of "forgotten items." Whenever I arrived with them, Ben would be coloring, and Louella would be grinning and waiting to whip me in some musty old game like Chinese checkers or Yahtzee that Miss Tippett had dug out from her closet stash. (Where's *Gameboy* when I needed him?) Louella knew the game was in the bag the day she pulled out an old Scrabble board. "No way, Word Woman," I protested.

"Better Word Woman than Walt Whitless," she said pointedly. No longer hidden by oily spikes, her eyes locked onto mine.

"Walt's a goner, Louella," I said. "We're good."

I took my drubbing, but it was still a win because I liked hanging out with her. Besides, I had a whole summer for rematches. I decided one day to get a whopping edge on her by bringing her to a nearby rec area to shoot hoops. Ben, meanwhile, was happily benched with crayons and a score sheet.

"Sure you haven't done this before?" I asked after watching her dunk her second straight shot.

"Nooo," she said panting and pushing the ball upward. "I feel klutzy, but I need this. In gym my teacher keeps telling me, 'Head high, Louella. Eyes off the ground.' " As I watched her study the net and stretch upward on her toes, I thought back to the downcast eyes.

"Then remind me not to take you *there*," I said pointing to a nearby soccer field.

She looked over and laughed. "My KICK ME days are over. No S·O·C·K H·E·R for me, ha, ha," she spelled out.

Scratch one-upmanship. Louella was looking up and lightening up, and that meant we both were on a winning streak. More hoop days would follow.

And then there was Ben. On one of my visits to Miss Tippett, he presented me with his drawing of Cisco. Circles with lines poking out weren't about to shake up the art world, but coming from a kid who at one time could not speak to me, let alone look at me, they were right up there with slam dunks and three-pointers.

Between the Cisco magic and the end of the school year approaching, life was good. At school the wall décor came down, the moods soared. Even Darryl, upon hearing the news that the building site vandals had been caught, had good reason to be upbeat. Better yet, his dad had been going to Alcoholics Anonymous. No more cover-ups. No more excuses. No more shutting out the world from his family's home life.

On the last day of school, Mole met Cam, Darryl, and me as we left the school grounds. He wanted to be a part of the happy hysteria that marked the first day of summer vacation, but it was more than that. He was pumped because summer meant more of our time for him. He was also celebrating the fact that he and his dad had convinced the school administration that he was ready to return to school in the fall, with four weeks of summer school thrown into the bargain. "Keep Buckley and that Louella girl away from him, and William will do fine," his father had told them.

"And, Mole, keep *you* away from me and *I'll* do fine. I pulled a B+ in English. Not bad considering where I was a few months ago," I said.

Mole smirked and gave me a weak high five.

But I was serious. Louella and I had already signed up for Miss Buckley's elective writing course for the coming school year. Soon I'd have to be convincing my parents to do whatever it took to assure me I wouldn't be put in any remaining classes with him.

"Friday's the day, dudes. Everyone up for carnival time?" Mole asked with that annual enthusiasm he reserved for the carnival's opening day. To Mole, as always, it was right up there with national holidays, and he assumed we were all going to observe it with him.

I looked at Cam. "Go ahead," he said. "Dad and I can manage the store."

Darryl uncharacteristically was signing up for soccer camp that day—his father's idea. It seemed he and his Dad were making up for lost time. It would have to be just the two of us, Mole in the flesh for a change and I.

Come Friday, Mole and I were back to being kids again. In spite of the scalding early afternoon sun, we flitted from ride to ride, giddy from the rush; five or six turns on the Whip where we were at the mercy of a giant cake pan that whirled us against its inside rim; the Matterhorn that sent us into free falls; three turns on the Belly Blaster that spun like a giant wind gauge; and no-nonsense swings that spun like the spokes of a rotating umbrella.

We stuffed ourselves with cotton candy and fried dough, and for variety, took turns at the ball tosses. And Mole, of course, had to see the two-headed snake and the rubber man.

After a couple hours, with our bodies begging for solid ground and a break from food, we began heading back home on foot. With crowds of carnival-goers added to the shoppers at a Friday sidewalk sale, the main street was packed with people.

Mole walked with determination, eyes straight ahead, setting his own fast pace while weaving through the slow moving crowd. Suddenly he broke away in a sprint, veering to the left so that he could step off the curb and hasten past those walking near its edge. He then hopped back on without slowing his pace while I hustled to keep him in sight.

When I pulled up behind him, he'd slowed to a walk. It was that moment he turned to me and uttered, "Watch this body check!" I watched in horror as Mole took off ahead of me and threw his hips hard against the back of Louella, sending both her and Ben sprawling to the pavement.

Tires screeched. I stopped and stood in stunned silence while people gathered and huddled over the two forms lying on the edge of the road.

Above the sound of Ben's pitiful cries, a voice rang out. "Come back here, you."

And another. "Who *was* that kid?"

I caught a glimpse of Mole streaking along the curb. Then, swallowed by the crowd, in an instant he was gone.

With people pressing in, I could not see Louella and Ben as they lay in the road, but the normal street sounds gave way to Ben's loud cries. An eerie silence settled over the crowd. A man pushed his way through and removed his shirt, bent over, and disappeared. Time stood still. Then a woman wedged her way through the onlookers. She too bent over to help and disappeared from view. Next the blare of a police siren sounded, and the car and siren came to an abrupt halt as the swarming crowd squeezed itself together to let them through.

"Back, folks, please," one officer shouted as a pair stepped out of the vehicle. Then came the blare and flashing lights of an ambulance.

Long minutes passed. Above the cries was the metallic thud of the ambulance doors followed by the short screech of the departing siren. After the breakup of the crowd, I watched those whom Mole had so proudly dubbed the "blue morons" drive away.

The end of the commotion on the street did not end the commotion inside me. Not knowing the condition of Louella and Ben was bad enough, but knowing I had a part in it was worse. I could barely stand the thought. I began picking out faces I knew from school—not faces I could put a name to but faces that were part of the daily traffic flow in the school corridors. Just what had these people seen and heard? A part of me wanted to stare in search of clues, while another part, heavy with shame, wanted to avoid eye contact altogether. After all, I had been with Mole all afternoon. I was right on his heels. He had called back to me.

Three girls were clearly staring at me and talking among themselves in hushed tones.

I felt sick, and it wasn't just from junk food, heat, and amusement rides. I hurried from the main street to the base of an old river bridge, hurling my guts out as I leaned against its brick wall.

Then I sat for awhile on the rocky ground and remembered when Mole and I had hidden out here too. It was after Alex had discovered Mole had swapped Alex's soccer trophy for a deck of eighty baseball cards. I'd never seen Mole so scared. "It was just a trophy," he'd tried to justify. "Alex told me that himself when he won it." But Mole's fear of punishment was never realized. By the time he arrived home several hours later, his family was more concerned about the missing Mole than the missing trophy. Alex had to apologize to *him*.

Finally I gathered enough strength to walk home. Tracey took a long look at me as I walked in.

"You look awful," she said.

"Too much fried dough," I replied as I bolted up the stairs.

"I ironed your shirt for work," she called up behind me.

On any other day I would have loved her.

Chapter Seventeen

WHEELS OF FORTUNE

Good thing my parents weren't home yet because I was an emotional mess. My panic mode would have been on their radar as soon as I walked in the door, and the grilling would have begun. I knew I had to split before they arrived, and I knew I had to work off the adrenaline that had me shaking uncontrollably.

I ran downstairs and grabbed a Powerade. Then, after a quick "See ya" to Tracey, I left a memo on the answering machine. "Ah—hey, Dad and Mom. I'm working the evening shift tonight. I'll be taking my bike and staying overnight at Cam's. Tomorrow

I'll be working the noontime shift again." Except for the bike part, it was all a lie, and I hoped the rattle in my voice didn't give me away.

I hid my ironed work shirt in the back of the closet, then pulled on my bike shorts and a clean t-shirt. I stuffed a jacket, change of clothes, and a towel into my backpack along with a wad of bills—the half of all my weekly earnings that hadn't been banked. Next I threw on my bike helmet and sunglasses, then charged downstairs and out the door before Tracey had a chance to ask questions. I headed to the garage and removed my dusty bike from its wall hanger. My trembling fingers clumsily worked the tire valves to pump up the soft tires.

Without losing another second, I hopped on my wheels and headed to the river rail trail which would swiftly take me beyond the town's limits. I looked forward to the level pedaling that I hoped would restore some rhythm to a life jerked around by the day's events.

The breeze that cooled me as I pedaled, plus the knowledge that I was incognito as I sped past other bikers and pedestrians, convinced me that I had, at least this time, made a good decision. I pedaled for an hour before arriving at a junction where the smell of food lured me to one of the local outdoor food stands. I bought a burger and Coke and rode them over to a park bench where I plunked down the food, bike, backpack and myself. A monument of a foot soldier stood nearby providing a backdrop of privacy. As I gulped down my burger, another cyclist, a girl who looked close to my age, pulled up. Without a word or pause, she sat next to me. I ignored her.

"You're a talkative one," the girl finally said in a friendly voice as she pulled a set of earbuds from her pack. I turned to watch her remove her sunglasses and prepare to clamp the headset to her ears. It was then that I noticed how attractive she was with her large brown eyes, honey hair, and tanned skin. Her shoulder sported a small tattoo of a butterfly.

"You want to listen for awhile?" she asked. Her voice was soft and pleasant.

"Not unless you have news on that thing," I said half-jokingly. The truth was I had no intention of returning home until I could get my hands on some local news. While biking, I had imagined tomorrow's newspaper with headlines like RUNNERS LEAVE TWO INJURED or SIDEWALK COLLISION NO ACCIDENT.

Headlines like these would surely keep me pedaling, and I'd have to "pull a Mole." First, I'd have to hide away long enough to make my parents really worry. Then I'd have to drag myself back and hope they'd be so glad to see me they wouldn't care if I'd committed the bank heist of the century. And yet, how could I think about doing *anything* Mole-like when I was so furious at him.

"You one of those news freaks?" The girl giggled. "News is depressing. You look like you could use something upbeat. How about The Demons?"

I leaned my head back and shut my eyes without a word.

"Anyone who doesn't like The Demons has gotta be weird!" she said teasingly.

Besides her good looks, I admired her frankness and her taste in music. Still, I wasn't in the mood for tunes ... *any* tunes.

"You really should try these," she persisted, taking off her earbuds and handing them to me. "The sound is awesome. I don't wear them biking because you never know who might sneak up on you. Passing cyclists—or worse."

"Or worse?" I asked.

"Hey, you know the kind of world we live in, especially if you're a news junkie. You never know who might creep up behind you. Thieves. Muggers. Kidnappers."

I thought of Mole racing up behind Louella and Ben.

"Is that why you have your rear view mirror attached to your helmet?" I asked her.

She smiled a sweet smile—actually one of those big million dollar smiles with perfect teeth.

"Hey, I guess I do seem a little paranoid," she said. "Just to show you that I *do* trust people more than you might think, I'm going to ask you to watch my bike while I go up and grab a drink and a hot dog."

"Sure thing," I said, happy to have someone trust me more than I'd been trusting myself. She disappeared behind the statue.

Soon the food, her company, and the much needed bike workout were having a calming effect. It was early evening, and the park with its green lawns and fountains lulled me into a decision to stick around awhile.

"So what's your name?" she asked with a steady look at me that I always had been taught to use as a sign of another's sincerity.

"Tod. What's yours?"

"Monique."

"Nice name." It sounded like it belonged in a love song. It definitely fit her.

"You from around here?" she asked.

"A little north of here. Barton. I'm here because I like to ride at night after work," I lied. *"And here because I can pick between a cheap motel or a beach bench to sleep on,"* I thought to myself.

"Biking's the best. What else do you like to do?" she asked.

"Oh, I like basketball—not that I play on the school team or anything. And gym workouts. And hanging out with friends."

The eyes remained fixed on me.

"I like the friends and gym part." Then a long pause. "Do you ever just people-watch and try and guess what people do in their private lives?"

"Can't say I do," I answered, wondering if in an odd way she was overstepping into my own mental world.

Her eyes shifted. "Look at that man over there with his wife and kids, for example. The one covered with tattoos. What do you bet he pulls an all-nighter with his buddies and then goes home and beats up his wife and kids. Then, out of guilt, he takes them out for a picnic in the park."

"And has a *Jesus Saves* bumper sticker, I suppose?" I smiled at her. "Just because he looks like a wall mural and has muscular arms doesn't make him a wife and kid beater," I added, "assuming they *are* his wife and kids. A little stereotyping going on here?" I chuckled inwardly at her naïvete, though it didn't matter to me. It added to her attractive innocence.

Monique laughed. "Maybe being a girl just makes me more cautious," she said.

She continued. "Do you see the woman over there who just bought ice cream for her two kids after waiting for a decade while they picked out what they wanted? The one who's leading them to the park bench like the Mother Saint of all child protectors? I know for a fact that a few minutes ago she had been screaming at them in her car. I heard her when I was standing in line. 'Shut up, you brats. Your blankety-blank father is going to hear about this,' she'd hollered." Monique gave me a self-satisfied look and added, "*You* can fill in the blankety-blank." We watched the mother casually wipe off the ice cream that had run onto the shirtfront of one of the kids.

"Yeah, you're right," I said. "Some people are just dumb and cruel. But tell you what. That ice cream looks good. How about if I buy us each one before the line gets even longer."

I felt a slight rush as Monique lightly brushed my knee with her hand in approval. "Mmm. That would be nice!" she said. "My favorite is black raspberry. And when you come back, I'll put some awesome music to your ear to help you forget the nasty lady." Another giggle.

"Now you can watch *my* bike," I said. I pulled out a ten from my backpack and headed over to buy the largest possible cones so we would have the longest possible time together before darkness set in and sent us on our separate ways. Neither of us was in any hurry to leave.

When I returned, I flung the two cones into a trash barrel. Monique was gone. Her bike was gone. My backpack, minus the money, sat crumpled on the ground with my stuff scattered—and the lady with the two kids was standing at a bus stop.

Chapter Eighteen

TAKEN FOR A RIDE

I looked up at the soldier monument. He stood ram-rod straight with his rifle and bayonet poised at his side and his eyes fastened on me. "Thanks a bunch, bud. Some defender *you* are." I wanted to give the statue a swift kick. My backpack got it instead.

"Oh, Monique—or whatever the hell your real name is—you are one slick chick."

I looked around with the thought of hopping on my bike and going after her, but a grid of paved paths lay before me, and there wasn't a sign of her anywhere. People around me looked clueless. They were into their own good times.

All of that stomach churning anxiety that I had pedaled away made a sudden return. Losing the money was bad enough—my first real earnings—a private stash of fun money, *my* fun—not Monique's. But worse was the knowledge that I had been fleeced. *"Oh, she was so slick. And I was so thick. Get off the rhymes,"* I told myself.

Darkness was approaching, and my bike didn't have a light. Without a bright moon it would be impossible to ride home on an unlit trail and dumb to try and navigate the busy streets. Monique could stiff me, but she wasn't going to give me rigor mortis. Staying in a motel was now out of the question. It would have to be a bench at the beach. Homeless people slept there all the time.

Long after darkness I sat and watched the tide come in. Less than seven hours ago I was reveling in the glitzy lights and sounds of the carnival. Now they seemed distant and long ago. Finally, huddled under my towel with my head on my backpack, I curled up on my bench with my bike tucked beneath it. Before drifting in and out of sleep, I was reminded by the rhythm of the waves that some things in life you can count on.

~~~

At daybreak, stiff, chilled, and damp, I sat up on my bench. In my fitful sleep, I had dreamt of Ben's cries. Now I woke to the cries of seagulls.

After I returned from a walk to the water's edge, I stopped at Mel's Variety and scanned the front page of a newspaper: *"Ah, that cloned sheep again. Hey, nice mug shot, Dolly. Keep 'em coming."* —— Then the headlines: **Preparing Pathfinder for Mars Landing** ——*"Eyes on Mars. Works for me."* **Personal ID Thefts On The Rise** —*"Hey, anyone want mine? It's free for the taking—unlike this newspaper."* I returned it to its pile after repeated stares from "Mel."

Climbing onto my bike, I caught my reflection in a store window. A helmet, bike shorts, and sunglasses do wonders. For an instant, Monique, not I, stared from the storefront glass. Like a ghost of the present, she flashed her million dollar smile.

"You sack of sleaze," I thought. *"I've preyed on a few too, but you'll never find me smiling about it."*

I took to the bike trail. My next decision would be a no-brainer. Penniless and not about to become a street beggar, I *had* to head home.

First I needed to make one stop.

Chapter Nineteen

FALLOUT

I pulled up at Louella's street and rode slowly on the edge of the road. All was quiet at her house, and all was quiet at Miss Tippett's. This wasn't exactly bike alley. I knew that soon I would be obvious if I either stayed in one place or circled the neighborhood. To buy some time I got off my bike and removed my tire "for inspection." As I was about to give up and be on my way, I heard the sound of Ben's voice. Louella's front door opened, and he led her down the steps. White tape covered his arm from elbow to wrist, and I made out a patchwork of band-aids and bruises from his forehead and chin onto his arms and legs. Louella too had bruises, but Louella and Ben were home, and they were walking. With some relief, I climbed back on my bike only to find my wheels turning as much in my head as at my feet. I wanted to do something. Now! How about a kid flick! Pedalling past the marquee of the Princess, I hoped for that Clifford dog or maybe Thomas and his train. *Scream* was the only show in town, however, and this time it didn't cut it. "Doing something" was postponed for now.

What I couldn't postpone, however, was my dreaded homecoming. When I arrived, my parents greeted me with, "Did you have a good time at Cam's?—I can tell you didn't get much sleep—What did you say your hours are today?"

Slipping back onto the home scene was too easy, but I wasn't relieved by a long shot. For one thing, I couldn't level with them. Someday I'd share the days' events with them but not now. After beating up on myself, I didn't need anyone else to add to the pounding.

I didn't say a word about any of Friday's nightmare to anyone. For the next few days I went to work at the store, trying to lose myself in chores while still listening and watching, but it was business as usual, and I wasn't complaining. In fact, maybe it was time, I thought, to shake off the past and casually move on.

Then, on the following Wednesday, Mole signaled to me outside the store window. I cleared with Cam that I'd be leaving for a while. Instantly Mole's smug expression ignited the spark. I knew I couldn't do much about the Moniques of the world right now, but I sure could try to do something about the Moles.

"You want to know something, Mole?" I lit into him after we had walked around a corner and away from the storefront. "After Friday's little sidewalk freak show, I won't even give you the dignity of calling you a smart ass. Talk about stinking up the place. You are the pits. Talk about greasy. You are slime. Sound familiar, Mole? Do you get it there, dude?"

"Whew! What's *wrong* with you, man? I guess you've forgotten what that swelled-up nose of yours used to complain about. I did you a favor. She got you in trouble. She *messed* with you, man. I did it for *you.*"

"A *favor,* Mole? Huh! You haven't a clue, dude. And "*messing* with?" That's *your* specialty. Hands down. If you really want to do something for me, start by not messing with Louella."

"You're whacked, man. You're going to let a smelly know-it-all that nobody gives a piece of crap for spoil a friendship? Nothing happened, Tod. I'll bet you a pizza she and the kid are OK with no more than a bruise and a scratch here and there. It was no more than, ha ha, a bump in the road for her. You hear me? Nothing happened!"

"Yeah right, Mole. You're only a little kid's worst nightmare. Then again, maybe that gives you a cheap thrill."

"Chill out, dude! There are no cops on my doorstep. And what if there were. No one can prove it was anything but an accident. Just a kid in too much of a hurry. Nothing will happen to me, and nothing will happen to you."

I wanted to punch his lights out, as dim as they were.

"It's all about whether you get caught or not isn't it, Mole," I snarled. "Well, hear *me*. It's not just about *me, you,* or *us*. Don't ever tell me again that 'nothing happened.'"

My muscles stiffened. In an instant, I grabbed the front of Mole's jacket with one hand, yanking him upward, eye to eye. My other arm, fist clenched, wheeled back prepared for the strike. Mole went limp. One look at me had told him he'd be on the losing end of this one. Not Mole's kind of place. I relaxed my grip, but not before giving him a token shove into the brick wall.

Mole paused, then adjusted his jacket. We stood in silence for a few moments except for the sound of my still rapid breathing.

Then came his trump card. "Look, when you've calmed down, I'll be back later to pick you up in Alex's car. I'm almost sixteen now, remember? I get the keys sometimes. Just you, me, and the Grand Prix, dude.

"You don't even have your license. Forget it, Mole. Not interested. Get Darryl to go with you."

"You've lost a friend."

"You've got it wrong, Mole. *You've* lost a follower."

I turned and headed back to work, glimpsing my image in the storefront's glass. I shuddered. Just moments before I had been within an arm's length of becoming a Mole.

Chapter Twenty

CRIES IN THE NIGHT

Later that evening when everyone else was in bed
and I was fixing a snack alone in the kitchen, the
phone rang. It was Cam. "Did you hear?"

My mind picked up only fragments of what he
was saying — *accident... Mole... Darryl... wet
road... jaws of life....* With eyes welling up and
my throat growing tighter, I gulped and hung up
the phone. I hurried upstairs and flopped on my
bed, pounding my pillow with my head and fists.

I wanted to sleep—forever—but my brain's screen
saver floated the words and images through my

head all night. By dawn the glowing numbers on the alarm clock and I were still keeping company.

The summer that began with lots of promise had suddenly become the summer from hell.

Chapter Twenty-One

IMPACTS

It was also a summer of *weirdness.*

To begin with, I wasn't used to waiting out matters of life and death. Both Mole and Darryl spent days in intensive care, and it seemed forever before doctors were hopeful about their recoveries. "William lost a hand," they said, "and Darryl's leg was shattered." Doctors couldn't say for sure that Darryl's walking would someday be normal. "Healing will tell, and that will take time. Lots of it."

My father and I, meanwhile, visited the scene of the crash. The banged up guard rail. The bark stripped from the tree. The shards of broken glass picked up by the sun's rays. And then the trip to the body shop where Alex's car, Mole's first trophy, sat in a crumpled heap with the front and driver's side so smashed and the inside so full of twisted debris that *lucky* was redefined. How did they survive it?

I wasn't used to hospitals either. At first only the bruises, stitches, swellings, casts, and huge array of medical equipment spoke for Darryl and Mole. I didn't recognize either one.

Gradually the medications lessened, and their recognition of the world around them returned. Yet they weren't the guys I knew before.

Now, almost every time I walked into Darryl's bright hospital room, it was a standing-room-only gathering of get-well wishers—his sober dad, his mom, his soccer teammates, other friends from school, lots of balloons and cards—all for a once so-called "weird guy" who liked to huddle in the background. I remembered with haunting regret— "Get Darryl to go with you." Darryl, my easy pawn and Mole's easy recruit.

It was an "accident" that didn't happen "by accident." Darryl could clearly remember the fierce pedal to the metal that had gripped Mole that night and the panicked shouts of "slow down." He could remember the hydroplaning. But Darryl was as protective of Mole as he once had been of his father. Darryl would only tell *me* about all that happened that terrible night since I promised him I would never tell anyone, just as I promised myself that I would never tell Darryl about my argument with Mole that day. Why should I? Our reckless ride began long before Mole and Darryl's date with disaster.

Each time I walked by Mole's dimly lit hospital room, he, the lover of attention, often lay alone, his eyes staring at the ceiling. Sometimes his parents and brother were at his side, his dad looking helplessly on. No balloons, card-covered walls, or audible voices. No Mole fans helping him on to recovery. And Mole himself, no longer a swamp creature ready to snap at some unsuspecting prey. Only the "hiss" of the hospital machines. I saw a broken body that weirdly seemed *less* fragile to me than when it was whole. No more hair-trigger impulses. No more delicate loose cannon. Just lots of time to think. Not a bad thing for Mole. I'd entered Mole's room only once. "We were a great team, and you sold me out, man," he said.

"To what, Mole? To what did I sell you out? The system?" I looked around at the doctors and nurses gliding through the hallway; then at the hospital equipment in his room—the monitors, the IV's, the maze of tubes. "I've got news for you, Mole. The system saved your sorry butt." I walked out and didn't go back.

As for what really happened that Friday afternoon? That was for Mole and me to know. I didn't even plan on telling Louella—not yet. Then again, she hadn't been around to tell. Miss Tippett still saw Louella and Ben. I did not.

"They were mowed down by a crowd of people," Miss Tippett told me. "Right on the main street. Plenty of scrapes and gashes, that's for sure. And Ben's cracked wrist. They'll have scars, I'm sure of that. And they'll have bills to pay, but I don't know with what." I winced but said nothing.

I preferred to chalk up the no-shows to Louella and Ben's needed healing time and summer's change of routine. Yet as difficult as it was to do, I also had to admit to myself that maybe Louella had the truth figured out. Not that she couldn't handle the truth, however. The "girl with no life" had learned to cope from the get-go. Tough-talking Mole was only now just learning what it was to cope.

Of three things I was certain. One, that come September, neither Mole nor Darryl would be heading off to school; two, that as long as Cam and I were on the scene, gator pits were history; and three, that Tracey's summer supply of peach ambrosia, compliments of me and Mr. Sullivan, would soon be history too. That was not a happy thought. And while I watched her stockpile tons of dorm stuff before moving on, others had *already* moved on.

It was in mid-August on one of my delivery days to Miss Tippett that I noticed the flashing marquee of the Princess featuring *101 Dalmatians.* Psyched, I convinced Mr. Sullivan to stop the van long enough for me to buy three movie passes, the invitations for Louella and Ben's "Let's Hang Out Again" party—kind of a pre-school party for Louella and me before hooking up in Miss Buckley's writing class.

But the party was over before it began. Instead, I stood with Miss Tippett on her porch in silence and looked out at a now vacant house with a FOR RENT sign in front. Fighting tears, Miss Tippett stammered, "It was so sudden. She doesn't even know where they are off to next. 'Too many liabilities' I think she said."

Another Louella-word, and this one I understood. I wished I didn't. Too many family debts? *That* I knew. And what follows unpaid debts? Usually eviction notices and quiet exits.

But Louella's liabilities went way beyond that. She was our chosen target, and we, her classmates, in a most shameful way, had found our mark. Not just Mole. Not just me, the fool who went along.

Not just those on the fringes who joined in "the fun." But also those who simply watched. She deserved our best but got far more of our worst, and there was no time left to settle the score. I'd miss her *big* time and not only because of our joint mission to buoy up Miss Tippett in her fragile years. Louella and I, we found out, could buoy up each other as well.

I decided in the coming school year I'd try out for basketball. If I made the team and gave up my job, (and if I had my way), I'd continue to restock one lady's groceries. Louella still had a part in that too. Miss Tippett showed me a cake that Louella had made for her before she left. Rather than eat it, she told me she was wrapping it and storing it in her freezer as an everlasting keepsake.

We kept our word. I continued to restock, and the wrapped cake never moved.

Epilogue

End of August, 2000

Summer haze has given way to clear autumn-like days, but what lies ahead for me right now is a blurry mix of excitement and anxiety. I am about to be a freshman again. The car is stuffed, idling in the driveway. Inside the house, my bedroom is stripped of nearly all but my two *"don't-even-think-about-touching"* items.

One is my basketball trophy—presented to me and my teammates at the end of our winning season in my junior year. What a ride!

The other is Miss Tippett's glass paperweight... and like Louella's cake, another gift frozen in time.

Its fixed underwater colony, with Ben's drawing of Cisco anchored beneath it, never moves from my desktop. Its message is always the same. The unique colors, shapes, and textures of its ocean reef did, and still do, speak of those unexpected discoveries we sometimes find, for better or worse, when we take the time to look beyond a surface.

The paperweight stays, but its message and its reminder of those "inspiring friends whom I will never consign to oblivion" go with me. These I can take anywhere, and I don't have to pack them.

Questions for Discussion:

1. For narrator Tod Whitney, new insight was acquired by a three way process that directed his attention: (a) to self, (b) to where others are coming from, and (c) to what lies beyond the surface.

   a. Why and in what ways did Tod surrender his own natural inclinations in order to conform to Mole's expectations?

   b. Which characters and events helped Tod tune into the needs of others?

   c. Paperweights are markers in the story, and each of their appearances marks an expansion of Tod's vision. Explain. What other items in the story helped to reinforce this theme of vision?

2. Mole prided himself on *physical* strength, and he worked out to achieve it. What other strengths did he have? What were Mole's weaknesses? Did the story suggest any reasons for some of these weaknesses? If so, what were they? Like Tod did, do you see Mole as a fragile person? Explain.

3. Oftentimes, the more self esteem one acquires, the less one is likely to become a victim of social cruelty. How and in what ways did Louella develop more self esteem as the story progressed? Even so, she and Ben still became victims at the end. Why?

4. Tod never revealed to anyone Mole's part in the street "accident" with Louella and Ben. Why do you think he did not? Do you agree with his decision not to? Why or why not?

5. Even though Tod befriended Louella, he still felt guilty about his treatment of her. Should he have felt guilty, do you think? Why or why not?

6. What other people became victims in the story besides Louella, the original intended victim?

7. What well meaning characters could have done more than they did to try and put a stop to the social cruelty? In what ways? If you were Louella, would you have done more than she did to advocate for herself? Whose responsibility is it to try and prevent social cruelty, do you think?

About the Author – Janet Morneau, a graduate of Colby College with a degree in literature, has taught reading, writing and literature to secondary students for 29 years. She currently lives in New Hampshire. *The Gator Pit* is her first book.

Questions? Comments? Send to:

gatorpitnotes@gmail.com

About the Cover Artist – The front cover was created by Lindsey Gillis, who at the time, was a sixteen year old high school student living in Maine.

~~~